Junie B. Jones
and a
little monkey Business

From The Chicken House

Everyone in the family (except perhaps little brothers) will get tickled pink with Junie's latest misunderstandings – but maybe she's right after all, and we don't think enough about our words. Now who called me a *couch potato?*

Barry Cunningham
Publisher

Junie B. Jones
and a
Little Monkey Business

By Barbara Park

Illustrated by Denise Brunkus

2 Palmer Street, Frome, Somerset BA11 1DS

The Junie B. Jones series by Barbara Park

First published in the United States in 1993 by Random House, Inc.
Text copyright © 1993 by Barbara Park
Illustrations copyright © 1993 by Denise Brunkus

This edition first published in Great Britain in 2006 by
The Chicken House
2 Palmer Street
Frome, Somerset BA11 1DS
United Kingdom
www.doublecluck.com

Cover design by Radio
Cover Illustration by Denise Brunkus
Typeset by Dorchester Typesetting Group Ltd
Printed and bound in Great Britain

1 3 5 7 9 10 8 6 4 2

British Library Cataloguing in Publication data available.

10 digit ISBN 1 905294 07 7
13 digit ISBN 978 1905294 07 7

Contents

Chapter 1

Surprise

My name is Junie B. Jones. The B stands for Beatrice. Except I don't like Beatrice. I just like B and that's all. B stands for something else, too.

B stands for B-A-B-Y.

I'm only in Reception. But I already know how to spell B-A-B-Y. That's because my mother told me that she is going to have one of those things.

She and Daddy told me about it at dinner one night. It was the night we had tinned

1

tomatoes – which I hate very much.

"Daddy and I have a surprise for you, Junie B.," said Mother.

And so then I got very happy inside. Because maybe I didn't have to eat my euwie pewie tomatoes.

And also sometimes a surprise means a present! And presents are my very favourite things in the whole world!

I bounced up and down on my chair.

"What is it? Is it all wrapped up? I can't see it," I said very excited.

Then I looked under the table. Because maybe the surprise was hiding down there with a red ribbon on top of it.

Mother and Daddy smiled at each other. Then Mother held my hand.

"Junie B., how would you like to have a

little baby brother or sister?" she said.

I made my shoulders go up and down.

"I don't know. Maybe," I told her.

Then I looked under my chair.

"Guess what?" I said. "I can't find that silly billy present anywhere."

Mother made me sit up. Then she and my daddy said some more stuff about a baby.

"The baby will be yours, too, Junie B.," Daddy said. "Just think. You'll have your very own little brother or sister to play with. Won't that be fun?"

I did my shoulders up and down again. "I don't know. Maybe," I said.

Then I got down from my chair and ran into the living room.

"BAD NEWS, PEOPLES!" I yelled very loud. "THE PRESENT ISN'T IN THIS DUMB ROOM, EITHER!"

Mother and Daddy came into the living room. They didn't look that smiley any more.

Daddy took a big breath. "There is no *present*, Junie B.," he said. "We never said we had a present. We said we had a *surprise*. Remember?"

Then Mother sat down next to me. "The surprise is that I'm going to have a *baby*, Junie B. In a few months you're going to have a little baby brother or sister. Do you get what I'm saying yet?"

Just then I folded my arms and made a grumpy face. 'Cos all of a sudden I got it, that's why.

"You didn't get me a bloomin' thing, did you?" I said very growly.

Mother looked angry at me. "I give up!" she said. Then she went back into the kitchen.

Daddy said that I owed her a 'pology.

A 'pology is when I have to say the words *I'm sorry*.

"Yes, but she owes me a 'pology, too," I said. "Because a baby isn't a very good surprise."

I made a wrinkly nose. "Babies smell like PU," I explained. "I smelled one at my friend Grace's house. It had some sick on its front. And so I held my nose and shouted, 'PU! WHAT A STINK BOMB!' And then that Grace made me go home."

After I finished my story, Daddy went into the kitchen to talk to Mother.

Then Mother called me in there. And she said if the baby smells like a stink bomb, she will buy me my very own air freshener. And I can spray the can all by myself.

Except not on the PUEY baby.

"I would like the one that smells as fresh

as a pine forest," I said.

Then me and Mother hugged. And I sat back down at the table. And I finished eating my dinner.

Except not my euwie pewie tomatoes.

And so guess what?

No dessert, that's what.

Chapter 2

The Stupid Dumb Baby's Room

Mother and Daddy fixed up a room for the new baby. It's called a nursery. Except I don't know why. Because a baby isn't a nurse, of course.

The baby's room used to be the guest room. That's where all our guests used to sleep. Only we never had much guests.

And so now if we get some, they'll have to sleep on a table or something.

The baby's room has new stuff in it. That's because Mother and Daddy went shopping at the new baby-stuff shop.

They bought a new baby chest of drawers with green and yellow knobs on it. And a new baby lamp with a giraffe on the lamp shade. And also, a new rocking chair for when the baby cries and you can't shut it up.

And there's a new baby cot, too.

A cot is a bed with bars on the side of it. It's kind of like a cage at the zoo. Except with a cot, you can put your hand through the bars. And the baby won't pull you in and kill you.

And guess what else is in the nursery? Wallpaper, that's what! The jungle kind. With pictures of elephants, and lions, and a big fat hippo-pot-of-something.

And there's monkeys, too! Which are my most favourite jungle peoples in the world!

Mother and Daddy pasted on the wallpaper together.

Me and my dog Tickle were watching them.

"This wallpaper looks very cool in here," I told them. "I would like some of it in my room, too, I think. OK?" I said. "Can I? Can I?"

"We'll see," said Daddy.

We'll see is another word for no.

"Yeah, only that's not fair," I said. "'Cos the baby gets all new stuff and I have all old stuff."

"Poor Junie B.," said Mother very teasing.

Then she bended down and tried to hug me. Only she couldn't do it very good. Because of her big fat stomach – which is where the stupid baby is.

"I don't think I'm going to like this stupid

dumb baby," I said.

Mother stopped hugging me.

"Don't say that, Junie B. Of course you will," she said.

"Of course I won't," I talked back. "Because it won't even let me hug you very good. And anyway, I don't even know its stupid dumb name."

Then Mother sat down in the new rocking chair. And she tried to put me on her lap. Only I wouldn't fit. So she just holded my hand.

"That's because Daddy and I haven't picked a name for the baby yet," she explained. "We want a name that's a little bit different. You know, something nice like Junie B. Jones. A name that people will remember."

And so I thought and thought very hard.

And then I clapped my hands together really loud.

"Hey! I know one!" I said very excited. "It's the dinner lady at my school. And her name is Mrs Gutzman!"

Mother frowned a little bit. And so maybe she didn't hear me, I think.

"MRS GUTZMAN!" I yelled. "That's a nice name, don't you think? And I remembered it, too! Even after I only heard it one time, Mrs Gutzman sticked right in my head!"

Mother took a big breath. "Yes, sweetheart. But I'm not sure that Mrs Gutzman is a good name for a tiny baby."

And so then I scrunched my face up. And I thought and thought all over again.

"How 'bout Teeny?" I said. "Teeny would be good."

Mother smiled. "Well, Teeny might be sweet while the baby was little. But what would we call him when he grows up?"

"Big Teeny!" I called out very happy.

Then Mother said, "We'll see."

Which means no Big Teeny.

After that, I didn't feel so happy any more.

"When's this stupid fruit loop baby getting here anyway?" I said.

Mother frowned again. "The baby is not a fruit loop, Junie B.," she said. "And it will be here very soon. So I think you'd better start getting used to the idea."

Then her and Daddy began pasting wallpaper again.

And so I opened the new baby chest of drawers with the green and yellow knobs. And I looked at the new baby clothes.

The baby pyjamas were very weensy. And

the baby socks wouldn't even fit on my big piggie toe.

"I'm going to be the boss of this baby," I said to Tickle. "'Cos I'm the biggest, that's why."

Daddy snapped his fingers at me. "That's enough of that kind of talk, Madam," he said.

Madam's my name when I'm in trouble.

After that, him and Mother went to the kitchen to get some more paste.

And so I looked down the hall to make sure he was gone.

"Yeah, only I'm still gonna be the boss of it," I whispered.

Ha ha. So there.

Chapter 3

A Very Wonderful Thing!

Yesterday a very wonderful thing happened!

And it's called – I had lemon meringue for dinner!

Just lemon meringue and that's all!

That's because my mother went to the hospital to have the baby. And Daddy and Grandma Miller went with her.

And so me and my grampa got to stay at his house. All by ourselves. And no one even babysitted us!

And guess what? Grampa smoked a real live cigar right inside the house! And Grandma didn't yell, "Go outside with that thing, Frank!"

Then, my grampa gave me a piggyback.

And he let me put on Grandma Miller's new hat – with the long brown feather.

And also, I got to walk in her red high heels.

Only then I fell down in the kitchen. And so I quick took them off.

"Hey! I could crack my head open in these stupid things," I said very loud.

After that, I opened up the fridge. 'Cos I was hungry from playing, that's why.

"HEY! GUESS WHAT? THERE'S A BIG FAT LEMON MERINGUE IN HERE, FRANK!" I yelled.

And so then Grampa Miller got down two plates. And then me and him ate the big fat lemon meringue for our dinner!!

Just lemon meringue and that's all!!

And we're not even going to get in trouble! 'Cos we're going to tell Grandma that her cat ate it!

And here's another very fun thing. I got to sleep in Grampa Miller's guest room!

First I put on my p.j.'s. And then my grampa watched me brush my new front tooth. And he tucked me into the big guest bed.

"Sweet dreams, Junie B.," he said.

Except for then I got a little bit of scared in me.

"Yeah. Only guess what, Grampa," I said. "It's very dark in this big room. And so there might be hidey things in here."

Grampa looked all around the room. And also in the wardrobe.

"Nope. No hidey things in here," he said.

After that he left on the hall light for me. So my 'magination wouldn't run wild.

Except I still didn't sleep that good. 'Cos

there was a dribbly thing with claws under my bed, I think.

And so this morning, my eyes felt very sagging.

Only then I sniffed something that woke them right up.

And its name was delicious pancakes!

Grampa Miller cooked them for me! And he let me sprinkle on my own sugar. And he didn't yell stop! stop! stop!

After that, me and him played until it was time for school.

Except before I left, the funnest thing of all happened! My grandma Miller came home!

And she said that Mother had a baby!

And it was the boy kind!

Then me and her and my grampa all did a big giant hug!

And Grandma Miller picked me up. And she swinged me in the air.

"You're just going to love him, Junie B.!" she said. "Your new brother is the cutest little monkey I've ever seen!"

Then my eyes got very wide. "He is? Really?" I said.

Grandma Miller put me down. Then she started talking to my grampa.

"Wait till you see him, Frank," she said. "He's got the longest little fingers and toes!"

I tugged on her dress. "How long, Grandma?" I said. "Longer than mine?"

But Grandma just kept on talking.

"And his hair, Frank! My word! He's got oodles and oodles of thick black hair!"

I pulled on Grandma's arm. "How come, Grandma? How come he's got hair?" I asked. "I thought little babies were supposed to be baldies."

But still, my grandma didn't answer me.

"And he's big, too, Frank. He's much bigger than any of the other babies in the hospital. And you should feel how tightly he grabs on to your finger when you—"

Just then I stamped my foot very hard.

"HEY! I WANT SOME ANSWERS DOWN HERE, HELEN! HE'S MY BABY TOO, YOU KNOW!"

Grandma Miller frowned at me. 'Cos I'm not supposed to call her Helen, I think.

"Sorry," I said kind of quiet.

Then Grandma Miller bended down next to me. And so I didn't have to shout any more.

"Are you telling me the truth, Grandma?" I said. "Is my brother *really* the cutest little monkey you've ever seen? For really and honest and truly?"

Then my grandma Miller hugged me very tight.

"Yes, little girl," she whispered in my ear. "For really and honest and truly."

After that, she picked me up again. And me and her twirled all around the kitchen.

Chapter 4

Hoppy and Russell

My room at school is named Room Nine.

I have two bestest friends in that place. One of them has the name of Lucille.

Lucille sits right exactly next to me.

She has a red chair. And also little red fingernails which are very glossy.

My other bestest friend is named Grace.

Me and that Grace sit together on the mini-bus. Except for not today we didn't. Because today Grampa Miller drove me.

Then he walked to Room Nine with me.

And he waved at my teacher.

Her name is Mrs.

She has another name, too. But I just like Mrs and that's all.

When I first walked into my room, Lucille was looking at that Grace's brand new shoes. And their name was pink high tops.

"Hey, Grace! Those new shoes look very beautiful on you!" I said.

But that stupid dumb Grace didn't even say *thank you* to me.

"Grace is angry at you," said Lucille. "She said that she was on the bus today. And you weren't even there to save her a seat. And she had to sit next to a horrid boy. Didn't you, Grace?"

Grace bobbed her head up and down.

"Yes, only I couldn't help it, Grace," I said. "That's because I stayed at my grampa

Miller's all night. And there's no bus at that place. And so he had to drive me here today."

Then I tried to hold that Grace's hand.

Only she quick pulled it away.

"That's not very nice of you, Grace," I said. "And so guess what? Now I'm not going to tell you my special secret."

That's when that Grace called me a pooey head.

Lucille held my hand. "*I* don't think you're a pooey head, Junie B.," she said. "And so you can tell me your special secret. And I won't tell anybody. Not even Grace."

That's when that Grace kicked Lucille in the leg.

And so Lucille pushed her down.

And Mrs had to come pull them off each other.

I put up my hand very polite. "I wasn't

26

27

involved," I said to Mrs.

After that, we had to sit down and do some work. It was called printing our numbers. Only I couldn't do mine that good. Because Lucille kept on talking to me, that's why.

"Come on, Junie B.," she said in her whispering voice. "Tell me your special secret. I won't tell. I promise."

"Yes, only I *can't*, Lucille," I said. "'Cos no talking to your neighbour, remember?"

Then Mrs snapped her fingers at me.

"SEE, LUCILLE? I TOLD YOU NO TALKING TO YOUR NEIGHBOUR!" I yelled. "NOW I GOT SNAPPED AT!"

Just then a boy named Jim said, "Shush," to me.

"Shush yourself, you big fat Jim," I said back.

After that, Mrs stood next to me till I finished my work. Then I got it all done and she collected it.

That made me happy inside. Because guess what comes after work? Something very fun, that's what!

And its name is Show and Tell.

Mrs stood next to her desk. "Who has something interesting to share with the class today?" she said.

Then my heart got very pumpy. Because I had the most special secret in the whole wide world!

I raised my hand way up high in the air.

"OOOOOH! OOOOOH!" I cried really loud. "ME! ME! ME!"

Mrs shook her head at me. Because I'm not supposed to go oooooh, oooooh, me, me, me.

She picked William. He is a crybaby boy
in my class. I can beat him up, I think.

"William?" said Mrs. "Since you raised
your hand so politely, you may go first."

And so then William carried a paper bag

to the front of the room. And he took out a jar of two dead grasshoppers.

Except for William didn't know they were dead. He just thought they were sleeping.

"Jump, Hoppy! Jump, Russell!" said William.

Then he tapped on the glass.

"Oi! Wake up!" he said.

After that, William started shaking the jar all over the place. And he wouldn't stop.

"WAKE UP, I SAID!" he shouted.

Then Hoppy and Russell started falling all apart. And Mrs had to take the jar away.

That's when William started to cry. And he had to go to the nurse's office to lie down.

And so then I raised my hand way up high in the air again.

Because guess what? My Show and Tell was *way* better than two dead grasshoppers!

Chapter 5

Monkey Business

Mrs called my name.

"Junie B.? Would you like to go next?" she asked.

Then I jumped up. And I ran speedy fast to the front of the room.

"Guess what?" I said very excited. "Last night my mother had a baby! And it's the boy kind!"

Mrs clapped her hands.

"Junie B. Jones has a new little brother, everyone!" she said. "Isn't that wonderful?"

Then all of Room Nine clapped, too.

"Yes, only you haven't even heard the bestest part yet!" I said very loud. "Because guess what else? He's a MONKEY! That's what else! My new brother is a real, alive, baby MONKEY!!!"

Mrs got a funny look on her face. And she squinted her eyes very tiny. And so maybe she didn't hear me or something, I think.

"I SAID I'VE GOT A MONKEY BROTHER!" I shouted real louder.

Then that mean Jim jumped right up from his desk. And he shouted, "Liar, liar, pants on fire!"

"No they are not on fire, you big fat Jim!" I said back. "I do have a monkey brother! You can ask my grandma Miller if you don't believe me!"

Mrs raised her eyebrows way up high.

"Your grandmother told you that your brother is a monkey?" she asked me.

"Yes!" I said. "She told me he has long fingers and long toes. And lots of black fur all over himself!"

After that, Mrs kept on looking at me. Then she said it was time for me to sit down.

"Yeah, only I'm not finished telling the children about my monkey brother yet," I explained.

"'Cos guess what else? His wallpaper has pictures of his jungle friends on it. And his bed has bars on the sides. But I'm going to teach him not to bite or kill people."

Then this boy named Ricardo – who has cute freckles on his face – said, "Monkeys are cool," to me.

"I know they are cool, Ricardo," I said. "And guess what else? Maybe I can bring him to school on Pet Day."

Then Ricardo smiled at me. And so he might be my boyfriend, I think. Except for there's a boy in Room Eight who already loves me.

Just then, Mrs stood up and pointed at me.

"That's *enough*, Junie B.," she said. "I want you to sit down now. You and I will talk about this monkey business later."

And so that made me giggle. Because monkey business is a funny word, I think.

Then I waved goodbye to my new boyfriend, Ricardo.

And I skipped back to my seat.

Chapter 6
Bestest Friends

Playtime is my best subject. I learned it my first week at school. Playtime is when you go outside. And you run off your steam.

Then when you come in, you can sit still better. And you don't have ants in your pants.

At playtime, me and Lucille and that Grace play horses together.

I'm Brownie. Lucille is Blackie. And that Grace is Yellowie.

"I'M BROWNIE!" I yelled as soon as I got outside.

"I don't want to play horses today," said Lucille. "I want to know some more about your monkey brother."

"Me, too," said that Grace.

Then Lucille pushed that Grace out of the way. And she whispered a secret in my ear.

"If you let me be the first one to see him, I'll let you wear my new locket," she said.

"Yeah. Only guess what, Lucille?" I said. "I don't even know what a stupid locket is."

And so then Lucille showed me her locket. It was a little gold heart on a chain.

"Isn't it beauteous?" she said. "My nanna gave it to me for my birthday."

Then she opened up the little heart. And there was a little bitty picture inside that thing!

"Hey! There's a teeny head in there!" I said very excited.

"I know," said Lucille. "That's my nanna. See her?"

I squinted very hard at the little picture.

"Your nanna is a shrimpie, Lucille," I said.

After that, Lucille closed the locket. And she gave it to me.

"Now I'm your best friend, aren't I, Junie B.?" she said. "And so I can be the first one to see your monkey brother!"

Just then, that Grace stomped her foot very hard.

"No you cannot, Lucille!" she squealed. "*I'm* her best friend! 'Cos me and her go on the bus together. And so I get to see her monkey brother first. Don't I, Junie B.? Don't I? Don't I?"

I made my shoulders go up and down.

"I don't know, Grace," I said. "'Cos Lucille just gave me this locket with the teeny

40

nanna. And so that means she gets to go first, I think."

That Grace stomped her foot again. She made a mad face at me.

"Pooey!" she said.

Except for just then I got a great idea!

"Hey! Guess what, Grace?" I said very excited. "Since Lucille gave me something beautiful, now you can give me something beautiful, too! And so that would be very fair of me, I think!"

Then that Grace started smiling. And she took off her sparkly new ring.

"Here!" she said. "I got it out of cereal this morning! See how shiny the stone is? That's because it's a real genuine fake plastic diamond."

Then she put some breath on it. And she shined it on her sleeve for me.

"Oooooh," I said. "I love this thing, Grace."

"I know," she said. "And so now I get to see your monkey brother first. Don't I, Junie B.? Don't I?"

After that I had to think a little bit.

"Yeah, only here's the trouble, Grace," I said. "Now I have one thing from you and one thing from Lucille. And so it's a tie."

Then Lucille quick took off her red sweater with the Scottie dog on it. And she tied it around my waist.

"Here!" she said. "Now I've given you two things! And so I'm still the winner."

"Oh, no you're not!" shouted that Grace. "Because I'm goin' to give Junie B. my snack ticket for today. And so she can have my biscuit and milk!"

"Excellent idea, Grace!" I said.

Then me and her did a high five.

"Oh, yeah?" said Lucille. "Well, then I'm going to give her *my* snack ticket, too! And so I'm still the winner!"

After that Grace looked all over herself.

"But that's not fair," she said. "Because I don't have anything else to give her."

And so I looked all over her, too. And then I jumped up and down again.

"Yes you do, Grace!" I said. "You do have something else to give me! And their name is your new pink high tops!"

That Grace stared at her feet. She looked very sad.

"Yeah, only this is the first time I ever wore these," she said really quiet.

And so I patted her so she would feel better.

"I know, Grace," I explained nicely. "But

if you don't give them to me, then you won't be able to see my monkey brother."

And so then me and that Grace sat down on the grass. And she took off her new pink shoes. And she gave them to me.

"Thank you, Grace," I said politely.

Then I stood up.

"OK. Your turn," I said to Lucille.

Only too bad for me. 'Cos just then the stupid bell rang.

Chapter 7

Some School Words

I wore my brand new things back to Room Nine.

They looked very beautiful on me. Except my new pink high tops were too big. And my feet were very sliding around in there.

Before I sat down I looked at Lucille's red chair. Then I tapped on her.

"I'm sorry, Lucille," I said. "But red is my favourite colour. And so I would like that chair of yours, I think."

Lucille looked very upset at me. "But red

is my favourite colour, too, Junie B."

I patted her. "I know, Lucille," I said nicely. "But you still must give it to me. It's the rules."

And so she did.

"Now I'm definitely the winner, aren't I?" she asked.

I made my shoulders go up and down. "I don't know, Lucille," I said. "That Grace said she might have some money in her bag."

After that, Mrs handed out coloured paper. And we cut out autumn leaves for the display board.

Autumn is the school word for when the leaves fall off the trees.

We sprinkled our leaves with shiny glitter.

Also, I sprinkled glitter in my hair. And I pasted some to my eyebrows.

Then Mrs confiscated my shiny glitter jar.

Confiscate is the school word for yanked it right out of my hand.

Just then, Mrs Gutzman knocked on our door. And she came into the room with our milk and biscuits.

"HOORAY! HOORAY FOR MRS GUTZMAN!" I shouted at her. "GUESS WHAT, MRS GUTZMAN? I GET THREE SNACKS TODAY! SEE? I HAVE THREE SNACK TICKETS!"

Mrs walked over to my chair. She stared down at me.

"How did you get two extra tickets, Junie B.?" she asked. "Did you find them in the playground?"

Then she took my two extra tickets away. And she held them way up high in the air.

"Did anyone lose their snack tickets today?" she said to the class.

"NO!" I shouted. "Those are my tickets! Lucille and Grace gave them to me!"

Mrs raised her eyebrows. "Lucille? Did you give Junie B. your snack ticket today?" she asked.

"Yes," said Lucille. "That's because she made me."

"No, I did not, you stupid dumb Lucille!" I said. "I did not make you!"

Mrs said, "Be quiet," to me.

She folded her arms. "Grace? Did you give your snack ticket to Junie B., too?"

Then that Grace started to cry. Because she thought she was in trouble.

Mrs tapped her foot. "Please come and get your snack ticket, Grace," she said.

And so then that Grace walked to my table in just her socks.

And Mrs made squinty eyes at her feet.

50

"Where are your shoes, Grace?" she asked.

That's when big fat baby Grace started crying very harder. And she pointed at her shoes.

Mrs peeped under my table.

"Junie B. Jones!" she shouted. "Why are you wearing Grace's shoes?"

Mrs sounded dangerous.

"Because," I said kind of scared.

"Because why?" said Mrs

"Because it's the rules," I explained.

Then Mrs bended down very close to my ear. "What rules?"

"The rules for who gets to be the first one to see my monkey brother," I said.

Mrs rolled her eyes way back in her head.

"Put your own shoes back on. And come with me, young lady," she said.

Then me and her walked into the corridor together. And she made me tell her what happened in the playground.

After that, I had to give Lucille back the locket and the sweater with the Scottie dog on it. And I had to give Grace back the real genuine fake ring from cereal.

Then Mrs wrote a note. And she said for me to take it to the office.

The office is where the boss of the school lives. His name is Headteacher.

"Yes, but I don't think I would like to go down there today," I said. "Or else my mother might get cross at me."

Mrs tapped her foot. Then she took hold of my hand.

"Let's go, young lady. March," she said.

And so then me and her marched to the office.

March is the school word for pulled me way too fast.

Chapter 8

Me and Headteacher

The school office is a scary place.

It has loud ringing phones. And a typing lady who is a stranger. And a row of chairs where bad children sit.

Mrs plopped me in a blue one.

"Wait here," she said.

"Yeah, only I'm not bad," I whispered to just myself.

Then I put my jumper on my head. So nobody would see me in the bad person's chair.

After that, I peeked down my long jumper sleeve. And I saw Mrs out of my hand hole. She was knocking on Headteacher's door.

Then she went in there. And my heart felt very pumpy. Because she was telltaling on me, I think.

After a while, she came out again.

Headteacher came with her.

Headteacher has a baldie head which looks like rubber.

Also, he has big hands. And heavy shoes. And a suit made out of black.

"Could I see you in my office for a minute, Junie B.?" he said.

And so then I had to go in there all by myself. And I sat in a big wood chair. And Headteacher made me take the jumper off my head.

"So what's this all about?" he said. "Why do you think your teacher brought you down here today?"

"Because," I said very quiet.

"Because why?" said Headteacher.

"Because that Grace couldn't keep her big fat mouth shut," I explained.

Then Headteacher folded his arms. And he said for me to start at the beginning.

And so I did . . .

First, I told him about how I spent the night at my grampa's house.

"We had delicious pancakes for breakfast," I said. "And I had five of them. Only my grampa didn't know where I put them all. Except I put them away in here."

Then I opened my mouth and showed Headteacher where my pancakes went.

After that, I told him how my grandma

Miller came home from the hospital. And she told me I had a monkey brother. For really and honest and truly.

"And so then I told the children at Show and Tell," I said. "And at playtime Lucille and that Grace started giving me lots of pretty stuff. Because they wanted to be first to see him.

"Except too bad for me," I said. "Because when we came inside, Mrs found out about the snack tickets. And then that stupid dumb Grace couldn't keep her big fat mouth shut about her shoes. And so I got marched down here. And I had to sit in the bad person's chair."

Then I smoothed my skirt. "The end," I said nicely.

Headteacher rubbed his head that looks like rubber.

"Junie B., maybe we should go back to when your grandmother came home from the hospital," he said. "Can you remember *exactly* what she said about your brother being a monkey?"

I scrunched my eyes real tight to remember.

"Yes," I said. "Grandma Miller said he was the cutest little monkey she'd ever seen."

Then Headteacher closed his eyes. "Aaah," he said kind of quiet. "Now I get it."

After that, he smiled a little bit. "You see, Junie B., when your grandmother called your brother a little monkey, she didn't mean he was a *real* little monkey. She just meant he was, well . . . cute."

"I know he's cute," I said. "That's because all monkeys are cute. Except for I don't like the big kind that can kill you."

Headteacher shook his head. "No, Junie B., that's not what I mean. I mean your brother isn't really a monkey at all. He's just a little baby boy."

I made a frowny face. "No, he is *not* a little baby boy," I told him. "He's a real, alive baby monkey with black hairy fur and long fingers and toes. You can ask my grandma Miller if you don't believe me."

And so guess what Headteacher did then? He called her, that's what! He called Grandma Miller right up on the phone!

And then he talked to her. And then I talked to her too!

"Hey, Grandma!" I said very shouty. "Guess what just happened? Headteacher said that my baby brother isn't a real, alive monkey. Only he is. 'Cos you told me that. Remember? You said he was a monkey. Really and honest and truly."

Then Grandma Miller said she was very sorry. But she didn't mean he was a *real* monkey. She just meant he was *cute*.

Just like Headteacher explained to me.

And so then I felt very droopy inside.

"Yeah, only what about all of his black hair? And his long fingers and toes?" I said. "And what about his bed that looks like a cage? And the wallpaper with his jungle friends on it?"

But Grandma Miller kept on saying that my new brother was just an ordinary cute baby. And so finally I didn't want to talk to her any more. And I hanged up the phone.

Then I bended my head right down. And my eyes got a little bit of wet in them.

"Rats," I said very quiet.

After that, Headteacher gave me a tissue.

And he said, "I'm sorry," to me.

Then he held my hand.

And me and him walked back to Room Nine.

Chapter 9

Pigs and Ducks and Stuff

Headteacher went into Room Nine with me.

Then he clapped his giant hands together.

"Boys and girls? May I please have your attention?" he said. "I would like to explain what happened during Show and Tell today. It's about Junie B. Jones and her new baby brother."

Just then that Jim I hate jumped right up out of his chair.

"He's not a monkey, is he?" he shouted very loud. "I knew it! I knew he wasn't a monkey!"

I made a big fist at him. "HOW WOULD YOU LIKE THIS UP YOUR NOSE, YOU BIG STUPID JIM?" I yelled.

Then Headteacher frowned at me. And so I smiled.

"I hate that boy," I said nicely.

After that, Headteacher took a big breath.

"Boys and girls, there's a good reason why Junie B. told you that her baby brother was a monkey," he said.

"Yeah! It was all my grandma Miller's fault!" I interrupted. "Because she told me that my brother was a *little monkey*. Only she didn't mean he was a *real* little monkey. She just meant he was cute. Only who on earth knew that stupid thing?"

Headteacher made another frown at me. Then he talked some more.

"You see, boys and girls," he said. "Sometimes adults say things that can be very confusing to children. Like what if you heard me talking about a *lucky duck?* You might think I was talking about a real live duck. But *lucky duck* just means a lucky person."

"Right," said Mrs. "And when we call someone a *busy bee*, we don't mean he's a real bee. We just mean he's a hard worker."

"Hey! I just thought of another one!" I said very excited. "A fruit loop isn't a real cereal fruit loop, either! It's just a boring old silly person!"

Then my friend Lucille put up her hand.

"I've got one, too," she said. "Sometimes my nanna calls my daddy a couch potato. Only he's not a real potato. He's just a lazy bones."

"Yeah, and I'm not a big pig," said my new boyfriend Ricardo. "But my mum says I eat like one."

After that, a whole bunch of other children said they eat like big pigs, too.

Only a boy named Donald said he eats like a horse.

And crybaby William eats like a bird.

Just then it was time for the bell to ring. And so me and Headteacher said bye-bye to each other. And I went to my seat.

Then I gave Lucille back her red chair. She was very nice to me.

"I'm sorry that your brother isn't a real monkey, Junie B.," she said.

"Thank you, Lucille," I said. "I'm sorry that your daddy isn't a real potato, too."

After that, the bell rang for us to go home.

And so me and Lucille and that Grace held hands. And we walked outside together.

Only then a very wonderful thing happened!

And it's called – I heard my mother's voice!

"JUNIE B.! JUNIE B.! OVER HERE, SWEETHEART. DADDY AND I ARE OVER HERE!"

Then I looked in the parking lot. And I saw her! And so I runned to her speedy quick. And then me and Mother hugged and hugged. Because I hadn't seen her for a very whole day!

Then my daddy got out of the car. And he had a little yellow blanket in his arms. And guess what was in that thing?

My new baby brother, that's what!

He was very teeny. And pinkish. Except

his head had a lot of black hair on it.

I touched it. It felt like fuzzy.

Just then Ricardo walked by. And he saw my teeny brother.

"Cool hair," he said.

I smiled very big. "I know it, Ricardo," I said. "And guess what else? He doesn't even smell like PU."

After that I got in the car. And I told Mother about Lucille's locket. And she said maybe I could get a locket, too. And I could put my brother's teeny head in there.

"Yes. And I would also like some pink high tops, please," I said very polite.

"Maybe," said Mother.

"Oh, wow!" I said.

'Cos *maybe* doesn't mean no! That's why!

And so then I lifted up the blanket. And I peeped at my baby brother one more time.

"So what do you think of him, Junie B.?" said Mother.

I smiled very big. "I think he's the cutest little monkey I've ever seen," I said.

Then Mother laughed.

And I laughed, too.

About the Author

Barbara Park says: "When I was in junior school, I used to dream about having a baby sister. In my dream, she would follow me around adoringly while I taught her everything I knew. Then – when she got big enough – we would join forces to overthrow my older brother, and the sisters would rule!

OK, fine. It was only a dream. But when I decided to add a new member to Junie B.'s family, I was surprised to learn that, unlike me, she wasn't happy about having a new baby around at all.

But what if it wasn't an *ordinary* baby? What if it was – a baby monkey? Yes, of course! She'd love that.

Come to think of it, I would have loved it, too. My brother wouldn't have stood a chance."

Read this next book about me. And I mean it!

The bestest girl is in trouble

The bus got very quiet.

And everybody kept on waiting and waiting for me to say the name of my job. Except for I just couldn't think of anything.

And so my face got very reddish and hottish.

And I felt like PU again.

'See? Told ja!" said that mean Jim. "There is no such job! Told ja! Told ja! Told ja!

After that I sat down very quiet, and I stared out of the window.

'Cos the sickish feeling was back inside my stomach again, that's why.

Me and my big fat mouth.